★ SPORTS STARS ★

IVAN RODRIGUEZ
ARMED AND DANGEROUS

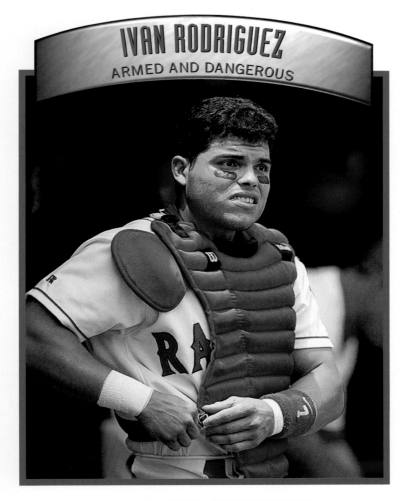

BY MARK STEWART

Children's Press®
A Division of Grolier Publishing
New York   London   Hong Kong   Sydney
Danbury, Connecticut

Photo Credits
Photographs ©: AllSport USA: 36 (Brian Bahr), 15, 20, 35, 44, 47, (Otto Greule Jr.), 25 (Rick Stewart); AP/Wide World Photos: 32, 45 right (Eric Gay), 22, 45 left (Ron Heflin), 18; Archive Photos: 39 (Reuters/Mike Segar); Corbis-Bettmann: 26 (AFP/Paul K. Buck), 11, 40, 41 (UPI); Sports Illustrated Picture Collection: 6, 23 (Ronald C. Modra); SportsChrome East/West: 43 (Michael Zito), cover; Tom DiPace: 3, 13, 29, 31, 46.

Visit Children's Press on the Internet at:
http://publishing.grolier.com

Library of Congress Cataloging-in-Publication Data

Stewart, Mark.
    Ivan Rodriguez, armed and dangerous / by Mark Stewart.
      p. cm. — (Sports stars)
      Summary: A biography of the catcher, Ivan Rodriguez, who joined the Texas Rangers when he was sixteen years old.
      ISBN: 0-516-21220-6 (lib. bdg.)   0-516-26485-0 (pbk.)
      1. Rodriguez, Ivan, 1971- Juvenile literature. 2. Baseball players—United States Biography Juvenile literature. 3. Texas Rangers (Baseball team) Juvenile literature. [1. Rodriguez, Ivan, 1971- . 2. Baseball players.]
    I. Title. II. Title: Ivan Rodriguez. III. Series.
GV865.R623S84   1999
796.357'092—dc21
[B]—dc21   99-23007
                                    CIP
                                      AC

GROLIER
PUBLISHING
1 2 3 4 5 6 7 8 9 10 R 08 07 06 05 04 03 02 01 00 99

CONTENTS

CHAPTER 1
Another Notch in His Belt   7

CHAPTER 2
A Boy Named Pudge   9

CHAPTER 3
Still a Little Kid   14

CHAPTER 4
The Gunslinger   19

CHAPTER 5
Coming of Age   24

CHAPTER 6
A New Beginning   30

CHAPTER 7
Back on Top   34

Chronology   44

Statistics   47

About the Author   48

ANOTHER NOTCH
IN HIS BELT

The ballpark is buzzing as the runner takes his lead off first base. He inches away from the bag, trying to read the pitcher's body language, trying to decide whether his next move is a throw to first or a delivery to the plate. The pitcher checks the runner and then fires the ball past the batter for a strike. The runner makes a move toward second base, then stops and begins to lean back toward first.

Suddenly, his nostrils flair and his eyes grow wide. He sprawls toward the base in an all-out dive. As his fingers strain for the bag, he hears the sickening *thwack* of the ball in the first baseman's glove, then watches helplessly as it slaps down on his outstretched hand, just inches from safety. "You're out!" yells the umpire, with a hint of a smile.

The Ballpark at Arlington erupts in cheers as the runner picks himself up and jogs back to his dugout. Ivan Rodriguez of the Texas Rangers has just picked another runner off first. No matter how many times he nails these guys, they never seem to learn.

A BOY NAMED PUDGE

The tightly packed cinder-block homes in the barrio of Vega Baja, Puerto Rico, do not leave much room for backyard baseball games. Still, seven-year-old Ivan Rodriguez and his father, Jose, found enough space to work on the fundamentals of hitting and pitching. Jose, a supervisor for a construction company, had been quite a player in his day. He had already taught the game to his first son, Jose, Jr. Now it was Ivan's turn.

Ivan's family struggled like most in Vega Baja. But neighbors always believed the Rodriguez children would make it, because they had excellent role models. Jose had a fine job; his wife, Eva, was a schoolteacher. And her brother was one of the most well-known painters in Puerto Rico. As for Ivan, he seemed like a dedicated, serious child. He was a good student who understood the importance of doing his homework and paying attention in class—even if he was terrified of being called on by his teachers. "I was very quiet," Ivan remembers. "I never raised my hand to answer a question. *Ever.*"

One place Ivan did not mind being noticed was on the baseball diamond. Baseball is the most popular sport in Puerto Rico, which has produced many major-league stars, including Roberto Clemente and Orlando Cepeda. In Ivan's Little League, there was an older boy named Juan Gonzalez. They played with and against each other over the years and became close friends. Ivan had a strong and accurate arm. This made him one of the better pitchers around. "No one could hit my fastball," Ivan claims. "It was fun seeing people strike out. I liked that."

Every child in
Puerto Rico (right)
has heard of Hall
of Famer Roberto
Clemente (above),
the island's
greatest
sports hero.

ATLANTIC
OCEAN

UNITED
STATES

Vega Baja
San Juan

PUERTO
RICO

Florida

GULF
OF
MEXICO

Bahamas

Virgin
Islands

CUBA

JAMAICA

HAITI

DOMINICAN
REPUBLIC

PUERTO
RICO

CARIBBEAN SEA

VENEZUELA

Soon it became clear that Ivan would not grow tall enough to be a professional pitcher. So his father suggested he try catching. Over the next few years, Ivan learned all he could about how to be a catcher. He would watch major-league catchers on television—how they moved, how they called games, what they did between pitches. One of the top "backstops" of the day was Carlton Fisk, whose nickname was "Pudge." Legend has it that Ivan took this nickname for himself, but that was not the case. Ivan says that, long before he thought about catching, a youth-league coach began calling him "Pudge." "I was kind of a small guy, a little fat," he remembers. "When they started calling me that, I didn't like it at all. Now everyone knows me as 'Pudge.'"

The Texas Rangers first heard about Ivan when he was playing in a Mickey Mantle League at the age of 15. He was already throwing the ball to second base at close to 90 miles per hour. The man who first notified Texas was the team's

Although Ivan admired Carlton "Pudge" Fisk, he says he did not take his nickname from the great catcher.

manager, Luis Rosa, who was also a part-time scout for the Rangers. After impressing the team again at a tryout the following year, Ivan signed with the Rangers. He reported for his first spring training in February 1989.

★ 3 ★

STILL A LITTLE KID

When people in the United States hear about professional baseball teams signing 16-year-olds, they naturally assume that these teenagers must be very mature. In fact, just the opposite might be true. If anything, Puerto Rican teenagers are less mature than their American counterparts. "Here in the U.S.," says Ivan, "I see 16-year-old kids working at fast food establishments, car wash facilities, and stores. That gives them an advantage in maturing and taking control over themselves. . . . I left my house at 16. I was still a little kid!"

Ivan may have been a kid, but he played baseball like a veteran. At his first spring training in 1989, he impressed the coaches with his skills, work ethic, and hunger to learn. He won the job of starting catcher for the Rangers' minor-league club in Gastonia, North Carolina, of the South Atlantic League and played 112 games. Ivan's second year in the minors was spent with Single-A Charlotte of the Florida State League. He made the jump easily, raising his batting average nearly 50 points and earning recognition as the league's top overall prospect for 1990.

Ivan dreams about advancing to the majors. He made it in just two years.

Ivan made progress with his English, too, thanks to a very special "tutor." Her name was Mirabel Rivera, and she was Ivan's childhood sweetheart. Mirabel had spent a lot of time in New York City as a girl and knew how to speak fluent English. The more time she and Ivan spent together, the better his English became . . . and the more deeply in love they fell.

Although Ivan already possessed major-league defensive skills, the Rangers did not want to rush their prized prospect. In 1991, they sent him to their Double-A club in Tulsa for more seasoning. In 50 games with the Drillers, Ivan hit well and threw out 25 of 37 base-stealers. Now quite confident that he would have a successful baseball career, Ivan asked Mirabel to marry him. She accepted, and the ceremony was scheduled to take place at home plate between games of a June doubleheader.

The day before the wedding, however, the Rangers called. Their catcher, Gino Petralli, had injured his back. Ivan was ordered to fly to Chicago and join the team for a game against the White Sox the following evening. The next morning, the lovebirds were standing outside the Justice of the Peace when the doors opened, and were married in a quick ceremony. Then they drove to the airport and hopped on a plane to Chicago.

The newlyweds arrived in the Windy City that afternoon. Ivan reported to the ballpark, quickly listened to advice about how his pitcher should handle the Sox hitters, and caught all nine innings of the game. He also gunned down two runners and rapped a two-run single to seal a 7–3 Texas victory. It was quite a debut! After the game, Ivan sat in front of his locker surrounded by more than two dozen news reporters. When a female reporter asked a question, Ivan realized that he had peeled off his uniform and was practically naked. He turned bright red and bolted into the showers;

his teammates almost died laughing. It was
the first time poor Ivan had ever encountered
a woman in the clubhouse!

**Ivan shows the ball to the umpire after successfully blocking
the plate. He was already an accomplished defensive player
at the age of 19.**

⭐ 4 ⭐

THE GUNSLINGER

Word spread quickly around the American League that 19-year-old Ivan was the new "gunslinger" in town. When the Rangers traveled to Oakland, everyone was prepared for a big showdown. The Oakland Athletics had Rickey Henderson, baseball's all-time stolen-base king. He was anxious to see what the kid had. The first time Henderson reached first base, he tested Ivan's arm, and Ivan threw him out by a mile. Henderson lay on his back in disbelief for several seconds before dusting himself off and trotting back to the dugout. For the rest of the series, Rickey stayed put on first.

Ivan's superb footwork and quick release enable him to get rid of the ball faster than any catcher in baseball.

Ivan appeared in 88 games for the Rangers in 1991, becoming only the second teenager in baseball history to catch so many games. He was aggressive at the plate and on the bases, and he played excellent defense. By the end of the season, few dared to challenge his powerful arm. Opposing coaches had timed Ivan and knew he would be tough to steal against. After a pitch reaches his mitt, a catcher needs to transfer it to his bare hand and throw it within 1.5 to 1.8 seconds in order to throw out a runner. Ivan consistently clocked in at 1.2 or 1.3 seconds. Unless a pitcher took a long time delivering the ball to the plate, there was no way to run on the Rangers.

Ivan could hardly wait to begin his first full major-league season in 1992. Though just 20 years old, he wanted it all, and he wanted it right away. "I wanted to hit .300, play in the All-Star Game and win a Gold Glove," he remembers. Incredibly, he achieved two of his three goals. Ivan made the All-Star team (the fourth-youngest player ever to

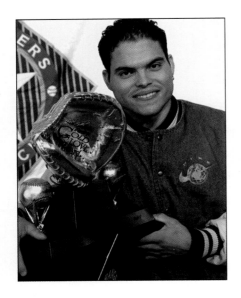

Ivan has had to make a lot of space on his mantel for Gold Glove trophies. He already has more than any catcher in A.L. history.

do so) and was awarded the Gold Glove for his fielding. As for his final average of .260, it wasn't .300, but it did rank fourth among American League (A.L.) catchers. Ivan also became the game's most feared pickoff artist. If a runner wandered too far off his base, the boy with the cannon arm could nail him without even coming out of his crouch. "If you're going to take a lead on me," he says, "I'm going to throw it. I'm not afraid."

Needless to say, Ivan's skills made him a popular player in Texas. But it was his willingness to get close to the fans that made him a special favorite. Ivan likes to communicate with the crowd during games. Once, while leaning over the railing to reach for a foul ball, he helped himself to a young fan's nachos. To this day, he makes sure to keep that connection alive. "Every single day after the game I stop and sign autographs," he says. "It doesn't matter if I strike out five times or make three errors—I always stay and sign autographs."

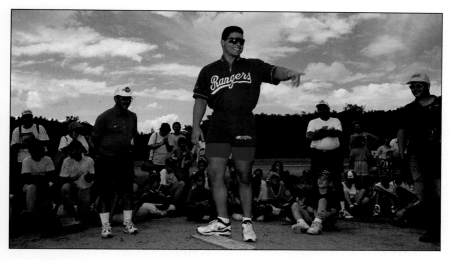

Ivan's fans gather around the pitcher's mound to hear him talk baseball. Most do not know that he started as a pitcher.

★ 5 ★

COMING OF AGE

The team that took the field for the Texas Rangers in 1993 seemed good enough to win the Western Division. In the course of one year, the Rangers had added slugger Jose Canseco and ace reliever Tom Henke. Former batting champ Julio Franco, injured in 1992, was back at full strength. And the team had a powerful nucleus in Dean Palmer, Rafael Palmeiro, and Juan Gonzalez, Ivan's pal from the Puerto Rican youth leagues. It was a lineup that scared a lot of American League managers. What terrified opponents most, however, were reports that

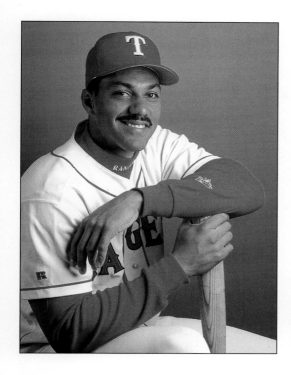

Juan Gonzalez, slugging star of the Rangers. Juan and Ivan have been Texas regulars since 1991.

21-year-old Ivan Rodriguez was starting to reach his prime.

As one team after another discovered, the rumors were true. Ivan hammered the ball all year long, raising his slugging average by 52 points and almost doubling his RBI total. Any questions about his toughness were answered when batter Hubie Brooks accidentally hit Ivan

Catches like this keep Ivan in the news, while making him one of baseball's most popular players.

in the face with his backswing and shattered his cheekbone. Three days later, Ivan was back in the lineup with a special plastic shield attached to his mask.

*   *   *

Texas fans loved their new star, but they
were getting frustrated rooting for the Rangers.
Once again, the team failed to win their division
in 1993. Worse, Jose Canseco destroyed his
elbow while performing a stunt: pitching in
a meaningless game. That embarrassment
was the low moment in a season that saw Texas
finish second behind Chicago.

Every year, something always seemed to keep
them from reaching the playoffs. The team had
entered the league in 1961 as the Washington
Senators, then moved to Arlington, Texas, in
1972. In all that time, the franchise had never
come within striking distance of post-season play.

In 1994, it looked as if the Rangers' luck was
beginning to change. On August 11, they held a
one-game lead over the A's, and were starting to
come together as a team. A division title seemed
within reach. Then the unthinkable happened:
a labor dispute between the owners and players
shut down the season. The two sides failed to

reach an agreement, and the rest of the schedule was cancelled. Even when the Rangers finished first, they could not make the playoffs!

Things were no different in 1995, as the Rangers sank to third place. The most notable thing about that season was probably Ivan's final at bat. Team president Tom Schieffer called him over from the on-deck circle and introduced him to Matthew, a five-year-old boy with muscular dystrophy. Ivan asked Matthew if he felt lucky. The boy nodded. Ivan asked him to kiss the bat so he could hit a home run, then strode to the plate and settled into the batter's box. Seconds later, Ivan sent a pitch soaring into the left field stands and circled the bases, pointing at Matthew the whole way around. No one in the ballpark that day will ever forget what they saw.

Ivan prepares to slide into home plate. Unlike most catchers, he is a fast, aggressive runner.

★ 6 ★

A NEW BEGINNING

As always, Ivan arrived at spring training in 1996 after playing winter ball in Puerto Rico. As always, he was enthusiastic about his team's chances. But there was something different about this group. All of the "parts" seemed to fit together perfectly—most notably the pitching staff, which was strong and experienced. The Texas offense featured a number of stars, including Will Clark, Rusty Greer, Palmer, and Gonzalez. This year, the Rangers' jinx finally ended. The team stayed healthy all season, the pitching held up, and the Rangers made the playoffs for the first time in their 35-year history.

Juan Gonzalez congratulates Ivan after a home run. In 1996, Ivan tied a record for catchers by scoring 116 runs.

The player who got most of the recognition was Juan Gonzalez, who hit 47 homers, knocked in 144 runs and was named A.L. MVP. But, really, Ivan had the "career year" at the plate. He had become a more selective hitter, letting a strike or two buzz by before swinging at the pitch he liked. The result was a .300 batting average with 19 home runs. In all, Ivan led the Rangers in five different offensive categories. He also made a

Ivan tries to fire up his teammates after tagging out Tim Raines during Game Three of the 1996 playoffs.

little history. No other catcher had ever recorded more at bats, scored more runs, or hit more doubles than Ivan did in 1996.

The Rangers faced the New York Yankees in the first round of the playoffs, and for a while it looked as if Texas's magical season would continue. The Rangers destroyed the Yanks in the opening game, 6–2. And in the next three games, Texas held seemingly secure leads in the middle innings. But the Rangers lost each of those games, as the Yankees always managed to claw their way back. Gonzalez was the star of the series, with 5 home runs and 9 RBIs. Ivan clobbered New York pitching, too, with 6 hits in 16 at bats. But the rest of the Rangers were shut down after the first game, and the Yankees went on to win the A.L. pennant and the World Series.

★7★

BACK ON TOP

After dipping to third place in 1997, the Rangers had a chance to return to the post-season in 1998. The Angels battled Texas right down to the wire, and with a week left, the two teams were tied. The Rangers got great hitting and pitching right when they needed it and swept three games against the Angels in Anaheim to wrap up the A.L. West and make the playoffs for the second time in three years.

Ivan had another excellent season at the plate. Early in the year he ranked among the league's top hitters with a .453 average, reaching base safely in 24 of his first 27 games. Ivan ended up

Ivan's 1998 season ranks among the best ever by a catcher. He batted .321 and threw out more than half the runners attempting to steal.

Ivan's hard work in the batting cage makes him a tough out. He had three hits in the 1998 All-Star Game.

leading the Rangers with a .321 average, which was also the highest mark for an American League catcher in nine seasons. His 21 home runs and 91 RBIs, meanwhile, were personal bests. He was practically a slugger! "I can't deny I like to hit homers, but I'm not a power hitter like Juan," Ivan says. "When the homers come, they come, and I will enjoy them."

Behind the plate, Ivan also had his best season ever. Besides fashioning a winning pitching staff from "spare parts," he threw out base-stealers at a higher rate—52.5 percent—than anyone since the statistic was first made official in 1989. Ivan received his seventh consecutive Gold Glove for fielding excellence, the most ever for an A.L. catcher. To top it off, Ivan was named to the A.L.'s All-Star squad for the seventh consecutive year. Clearly, he was the best all-around catcher in baseball.

The Rangers met the Yankees again in the first round of the playoffs. This time, instead of a slugfest, the experts were predicting a tight pitching battle. Unfortunately for Texas, New York's pitching was just a tiny bit better. The Rangers were held scoreless in two of three games, and lost the series 3–0. Once again, the Yankees went on to win the World Series. When it was all over, and the anger began to fade away, Ivan realized that they had been beaten by a better team. The main difference? Experience. As far as Ivan is concerned, that is something the Rangers will have the next time they do battle in the post-season.

Still in his prime years, Ivan has already earned a place in history as one of baseball's best all-around catchers. His footwork, fielding, throwing, and pitch-calling is unmatched in the game today, and he ranks among the toughest

Blocking the plate is one of Ivan's specialties. Derek Jeter of the Yankees watches as the umpire calls him out.

outs among hitters at any position. Yet he truly believes that he has something to learn—and something to prove—every time he steps on the field.

Some compare Ivan to Roy Campanella, one of the first catchers to combine clutch hitting with excellent defense.

"People say I'm the best," says Ivan. "But I don't feel like that. I feel like I've got to do my job—I've got to go to the baseball field and play the game 27 outs hard . . . that's why people like the way I play."

Is Ivan Rodriguez really one of the all-time greats? Old-timers are always the hardest to please, but if you ask them, you are likely to get a big thumbs-up. Indeed, they are nearly unanimous in their praise for Ivan. Those who saw Hall of Famers Roy Campanella, Yogi Berra, and Johnny Bench in their prime years say Pudge is right up there with them. And don't forget, he has a long way to go before he hangs up his spikes. His record is hardly complete.

Johnny Bench, whose record of 10 Gold Gloves once seemed unbreakable until Ivan came along

In fact, if you ask Ivan, he will tell you: "I think I can get better!"

That is good news for the Rangers—who recently signed him to a long-term contract—and bad news for baseball's base-stealers. Ivan has been making them look bad for nearly a decade. The thought of Pudge beefing up his game is enough to make them give up their "life of crime" and find less hazardous work.

Already one of the all-time greats, Ivan has a chance to make history. No catcher has ever reached 2,500 hits. Will Ivan be the first?

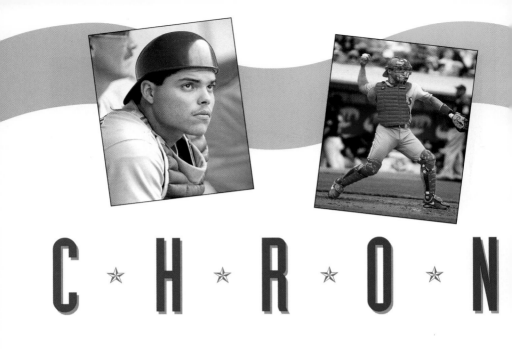

C ★ H ★ R ★ O ★ N

1971 • Ivan Rodriguez is born in Vega Baja, Puerto Rico.

1988 • At age 16, Ivan is signed to a professional contract by the Texas Rangers.

1990 • Ivan is named the top prospect by managers in the Florida State League.

1991 • Ivan gets married and makes his major-league debut for the Rangers on the same day, June 20.

1992 • Ivan becomes the fourth-youngest player to appear in an All-Star Game and is the youngest player in the major leagues for the second straight year.

1993 • A highlight of Ivan's season is getting on base in eight consecutive at bats from July 26 to 28.

1994 • Ivan leads all A.L. catchers in batting average (.298).

O ⋆ L ⋆ O ⋆ G ⋆ Y

1996
- Ivan and the Rangers make the playoffs for the first time in franchise history, and Ivan's season features a 19-game hitting streak.

1997
- Ivan signs a new long-term contract with the Rangers and then sets a team record for catchers with 20 home runs. His sixth straight Gold Glove award ties the A.L. record for catchers.

1998
- Ivan wins his seventh straight Gold Glove award and helps lead the Rangers to the playoffs for the second time in three years. He posts the Rangers' highest batting average (.321), and plays in his seventh straight All-Star game (most in Rangers' history).

1999
- On April 13, Ivan knocks in an incredible 9 runs in one game in Seattle.

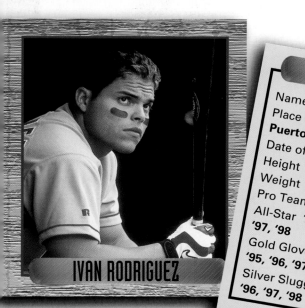

IVAN RODRIGUEZ

MAJOR LEAGUE STATISTICS

Season	Team	H	R	2B	HR	RBI	AVG
1991	Rangers	74	24	16	3	27	.264
1992	Rangers	109	39	16	8	37	.260
1993	Rangers	129	56	28	10	66	.273
1994	Rangers	108	56	19	16	57	.298
1995	Rangers	149	56	32	12	67	.303
1996	Rangers	192	116	47	19	86	.300
1997	Rangers	187	98	34	20	77	.313
1998	Rangers	186	88	40	21	91	.321
Totals	(8 seasons)	1,134	533	232	109	508	.295

ABOUT THE AUTHOR

Mark Stewart has written hundreds of features and more than fifty books about sports for young readers. A nationally syndicated columnist ("Mark My Words"), he lives and works in New Jersey. For Children's Press, Stewart is the author of more than twenty books in the Sports Stars series, including biographies of other baseball greats Mark McGwire, Bernie Williams, Ken Griffey, Jr., Kenny Lofton, Ramon Martinez, and Randy Johnson. He is also the author of the Watts History of Sports, a six-volume history of auto racing, baseball, basketball, football, hockey, and soccer.